For the curious child in all of us
G. C.

For my family
S. T.

A Lothian Book
Hardback edition first published in Australia and New Zealand 1997
by Hachette Australia
Level 17, 207 Kent Street, Sydney NSW 2000
www.hachettechildrens.com.au

Paperback edition published 2003
Reprinted 2008, 2010, 2014, 2016
This revised edition published 2012

20 19 18 17 16 15 14 13 12

Text copyright © Gary Crew 1997, 2012
Illustrations copyright © Shaun Tan 1997
Revised design by Shaun Tan 2012

National Library of Australia
Cataloguing-in-Publication data:

Crew, Gary, 1947-
The viewer / Gary Crew; illustrated by Shaun Tan.
978 0 7344 1189 1 (pbk.)
For primary children.
Regression (Civilization) – Juvenile fiction.
End of the world – Juvenile fiction.
Tan, Shaun.
A823.3

Colour reproduction by Hell Colour
Printed in China by Toppan Leefung Printing Limited

THE VIEWER

GARY CREW & SHAUN TAN

LOTHIAN
Children's Books

Tristan was curious from birth.

This is not to say that he was different from other babies; in fact he was rather ordinary. But from the moment he opened his eyes, he seemed to be examining the world.

As he grew older, Tristan would wander from his parents' house, to be found – hours later, miles away, and always alone – staring up at a cloudless sky, gathering autumn leaves in a city park, or crouched by the seashore, peering at some long-dead life form washed up there.

One place attracted Tristan more than any other. The city dump
stretched over acres of drifting sand, a vast crescent littered
with the detritus of a careless people. But to Tristan,
the dump was nothing short of a museum.

Every afternoon he searched for interesting objects to take
back to his room until curiosity led him to examine them
again, as if they might reveal another world.

One afternoon, as Tristan scavenged through piles of rubbish, he came upon the most remarkable find of all: a curious box. Fashioned from dark wood and burnished metal, and covered with detailed engravings, its lid was locked tight. Tristan ran his fingers over indecipherable names and patterns, sensing fascination and dread. He picked the box up and carried it home.

Later that evening, Tristan left the dinner table early, eager to return to his room to figure out how to unlock the box. Yet the moment he placed it on his desk, the latch snapped open. He carefully raised the lid. The musty odour of entombed air escaped from the dark space inside.

Tristan's pulse raced. The box was crammed with intriguing treasures, though all were devices designed to magnify, or focus, or illuminate.

What attracted Tristan most was an object that appeared to be an
old toy, a simple machine that a child might use to view pictures.
He picked it up and held it to his eyes. It fitted perfectly, as if custom-made,
yet through the machine's tiny lenses, he could see nothing.

Searching the deeper recesses of the box, Tristan found three disks of thin
metal, each framing a circle of black glass windows – each of them empty.
He inserted the first disk into the machine, and held it to his eyes.
Still nothing.

He pressed a lever at the side.
From somewhere deep within a light began to burn.
A delicate machinery clattered and chimed.
The disk began to turn…

One by one strange images flickered into life . . . At first a scene of fearful chaos . . . Then others, more luminous and eerie . . .

These sights left Tristan terribly afraid. After removing the third and final disk,
he put the machine away. In bed, he descended into a restless sleep, all the while
unable to dismiss the feeling of another presence in the room.

The next morning, Tristan could not stop glancing toward the machine, even as he
left to go downstairs. It sat upright on his desk as if staring back at him
– surely just as he had left it the night before?

At school he could not concentrate. He stared all day at the clock, observing its slow,
ticking circles, its relentless counting. He could only think about being back
in his room, looking into that curious world of images.

That evening, he lifted the cold eyes of the machine to his own, and inserted
the first disk again. He pressed the lever. The mechanism whirred and clicked.
The light began to burn – and Tristan gasped. The images had changed …

Afraid, Tristan wanted to pull the machine from his eyes, but something compelled him, against his own wishes, against his own common sense, to slip into the space between one flickering darkness and the next . . . drifting into a collapsing circle of time, that moment, the eternal present . . . returning, perhaps, to a place he had always known . . .

In the morning, when Tristan had not come to breakfast,
his mother called him. There was no answer.

When she opened the bedroom door the musty odour of entombed air spilled into
the hall. Tristan's bed was empty, the room unusually neat and tidy.
As if he had never been there … As if he had never existed …
As if things had always been this way.

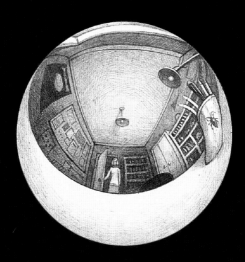

The only thing that seemed out of place was a box of dark wood
and burnished metal on his desk, its lid locked.

Curious, she thought.

And forgetting why she had come to the room,
she returned to her breakfast.

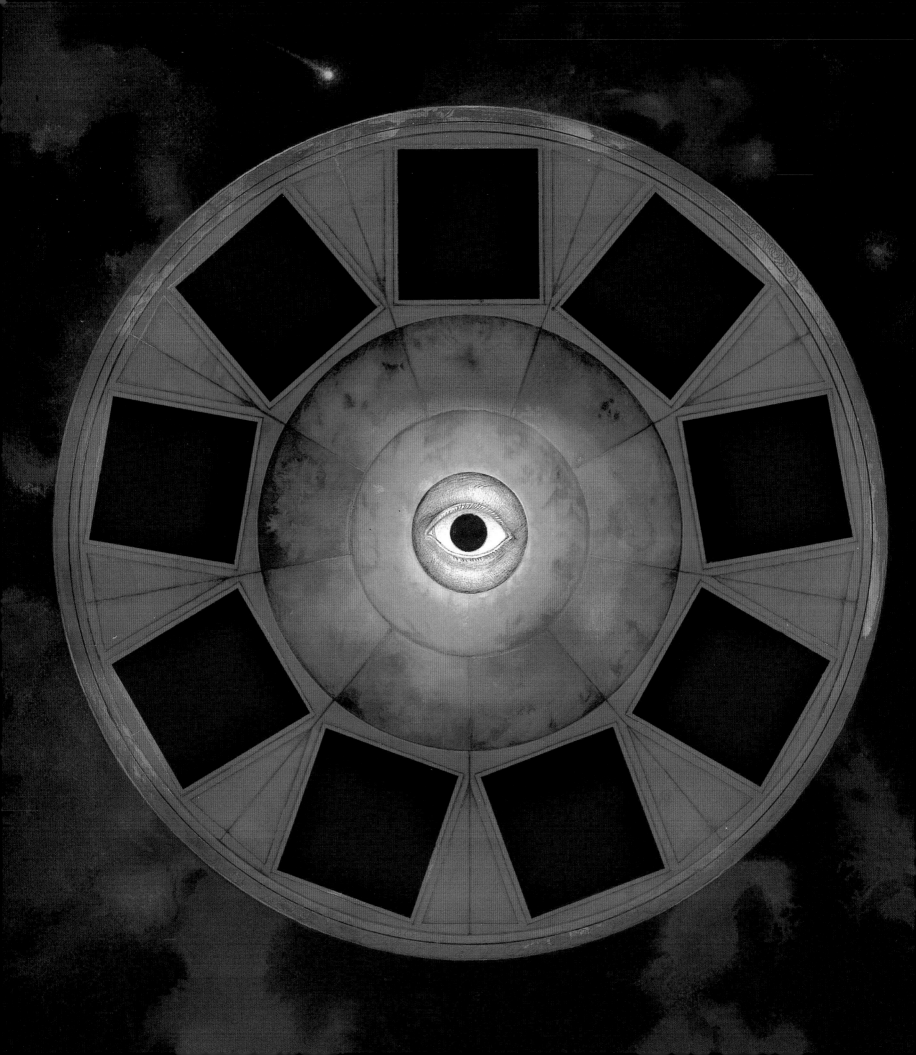

NOTES FROM THE CREATORS

During the 1980s and early 1990s I began collecting old toys. Perhaps I did this because I wanted my son to have what my parents couldn't afford for me. Who knows? Among these toys was one known as a 'Viewmaster', an optical toy into which the child viewer inserted a rotating disk of sequential, often historical images. One day, as I looked through this viewer, I noticed that an image in the disk sequence was missing. Had someone been here before and passed through into history?

Gary Crew, Maleny, 2011

I first met Gary Crew in Perth in 1996, after we had worked together at a distance on a series of stories called After Dark. As a young illustrator, I was intrigued by Gary's previous experiments in illustrated fiction, as well as a new idea for a story about an ancient device that records the collapse of various civilisations: a kind of visual 'black box' of human history, existing for an unknown purpose. A very strange concept, an unconventional narrative, and an especially challenging assignment for a first-time picture book illustrator! I think the result is as much a curiosity as its subject: an intentionally disjointed story without any moral message or clear conclusion, leaving the reader to puzzle over its meaning. Perhaps there might be moments in the distant future when this book is found languishing on a dusty shelf or within a pile of long-forgotten junk, when it still invites some passing interest before its inevitable return, like so many other things, to a long and silent darkness.

Shaun Tan, Melbourne, 2011